To: ....

From: ....

MR. MEN **LITTLE MISS**

GROSSET & DUNLAP
An Imprint of Penguin Random House LLC, New York

Published in the United States of America in 2020 by Grosset & Dunlap,
an imprint of Penguin Random House LLC, New York. GROSSET & DUNLAP is a trademark
of Penguin Random House LLC. Manufactured in China.

Visit us online at www.penguinrandomhouse.com.

www.mrmen.com

The publisher does not have any control over and does not assume any
responsibility for author or third-party websites or their content.

ISBN 9780593094174   10 9 8 7 6 5 4 3 2 1

MY SISTER

and me

by Roger Hargreaves

Grosset & Dunlap

My sister is always
excited and ready for fun.

My sister loves to play and jump and bounce around.

But this can sometimes
lead to accidents!

My sister can be a bit sassy.

But she is also really clever.

And other times, we are very different.

My sister makes a lot of mess.

But she doesn't mind cleaning her room.

My sister is very brave.
She jumps to the rescue
when I'm in trouble.

But she can get scared
and sometimes hides.

My sister has a big sunny smile.

And she tells lots of funny jokes.

My sister loves to play tricks on me.

But we always make
up with a big hug.

My sister has lots of friends.

And she loves parties!

My sister is a very good dancer.

She might be super famous one day.

My sister can be very grown-up.

And she knows the answer to nearly all my questions!

But sometimes I think
she gets carried away.

My sister is my partner in crime.

She is the **best** in the world.

MY SISTER

My sister is most like **LITTLE MISS** ....

I love it when she helps me to ....

....

My sister and I both like ....

....

My sister is very good at ....

....

If she were famous, it would be for...

....

My sister likes to read ....

The last trick my sister played on me was...............................

....

My sister is the best because..

....

This is a picture of
my sister and me:

by ....

age ....